Monday.

Bald Vision of Schizophrenia.

Made in Poland, hard work with taxes. There is no bank in the eye of he camera, so let's smoke viadro pokoju/ a peace bucket. Camp found on my way home long, long time ago. A year and half. So, for a witch, it's not so long, if she can live forever and play drums sometimes. Buying drinks is allowed for divorced ladies from Bearpitt. Vote for a picture of ART who become politic for us and them. Taking drugs to survive till morning to meet the ghost of the big creator. His finger or leg or an eye of Babylon – to possess the right Stones. Not cheap. No escape. Richest with Banksy and the secret garden on a roundabout and nun the guide to cat's tomb house. Mice not allowed nor rats. No rat or a mouse in da house.

Music through veins to the stinky sock with red. Fun with the sun outside.

'Do you smoke fags?'

'With pleasure, you want a roll-up?'

'Certainly.'

'Better quit roll-ups for weed, it's accepted by new system - Asystem – to find yourself in deep tension of surprises with evolution.'

'It's like an electrified cosystem schizów wypychanych do akcji, bo kamera działa/to push the button and translate for original polish volume.'

'Oh, I can see no evil except some symptoms of suffering an after death experience. To jump into real psychosis, when, after life you can find another life instantly, then you realise you find some kind of love and opera section instead of hiphop music.'

'True, false. Don't exist, but follow the eye of Superplant – to stay alive until morning – to save the world!'

'Only science can save us from hell – no faith in Jah – the soundsystem of the street, jungle, industrial, post punk & dread.'

Please take a seat on a sleeping bag and share a bottle of green light.

'Who took it?'

'Where is my roll-up?'

'This is hell to have a smoke and no lighter or matches.'

'I will try not to jump off the wall – to carry on the smooth side of the surface with some psycho experience.'

'Oh, bullshit, you saying madness for the masses, innit?'

'Yes, wicked vision on a whole packet of pills and MDMA. Always high, but who cares. Just a little line on Bearpitt, there is the best. We think it's a new wave of artists of life without a rebellion, but some love for past music and a strong accent on raegge, but to play on a radio station.'

'I don't like to wake up without a morning radio station – but what to chose where everywhere they are telling suspicious thoughts?'

'I've just seen the best lesbian porno in my life, so it's true that I can't see nothing better?'

'What if Leia got the voice to use magic, but she lives in a cave of sounds and visions? To tell her a locker and to rest for couple of days.'

'Yeah, yeah to lock and isolate a sick mind like the others.'

'So why this is a house where live thoughts are an invasion to build a new system which doesn't exist yet, but is said and done? To pick up chicks until will find love or lust? I'm already lost in Bearpitt.'

'Take a bath on Saturday night out or not? To shave head and say a name, but no-one remembers?'

People just passing by like British gypsies. All around here are travellers and scientists and healers to serve us, recover and refurbish empty souls. The house is flying above the land so we pay only a fee for electricity and running floor. Like at a school for witches, who live together for special reasons, to meet each other not just the once. No games on TV today. So late that it's a Monday morning. After 3 a.m. Ready to work on early shift and night shifts, plus noon breakfast with Marks & Spencer.

'I don't think so, it's too expensive for old English settlers. But there used to be a castle and brewery there. It was a home of kinky shoes. Like a surgery in Boots. Just to find the right floor - it's not quick if you are mental. Revolution become real, like a fighter in a ring. The war is over?! This December will be another John Lennon shooting anniversary.'

'I know, this is a Liverpudlian accent? So, why do all foreigners understand it easily?'

'Don't know, just Yoko Ono broke the code of connection. She was a witness and is still a widow. White widow plant.'

'I've got a seed of a cherry from Sheffield. I had a nice conversation with a doctor on my way from Hull. The train maintained my dreads without a needle. No need for heroin anymore. Just can't get no satisfaction!'

'Don't know what you talking about...'

'It's useless if you are not crazy and care too much about the meaning of money and order.'

'Disorder of puzzles and poor racing.'

Tuesday. Night shift staff.

Ignorant and Debenhams. Just watching the site on cam. So it's easy to bring a bucket on site in a red bag with a double-decker inside to hide the drug for healing. Smoke with fire and wind powers to change a building's construction.

We will put some pics on Facebook later. This picture of mine is so cool! Shining like a pigeon or a seaghull invasion. But this sparrow has got the power of love action. It's free to fly over ground control where the police are invisible, just watching the game from above, with the eye. Like a pyramid made by alien ancestors. I have some good titles from the closet. To find a treasure on an island. Can't hide from rasta & respect of street dealer. To just say high and hello.

'Smoke it easily girls.'

'With tops on it?'

'Yes sister, Jah!'

'Maintain dreads like plants.'

Brother with samsara in a pocket, but don't check the poor weed. The rest of it is just junk for stupid kids or amateurs of consumption.

'Can you take off your glasses?'

'Of course – you will see my warm eyes, outside of the system controlled by government and authority. Like a rebel in a city of greens and music.'

'I'm waiting for help and a flat in Bristol.'

'Happy hour in council…'

We are waiting until noon to appear at the meeting with the council. Too late, the meeting was yesterday.

'So what?'

'A lot. It's like English film about a dreamer's ball. Unconscious women in a hell full of doors and they feel lost, but find a garden with plants and a moon shadow, and the light found only to loose a grinder.'

'My bike was stolen in July. It's the first day of September. Go back to school like a proper teacher, why not?'

'I've lost my papers, it's all unreal without ganja.'

'Hope we don't lose anything during a last trip to the third circle of hell in town.'

'Wicked, I was pretending to be homeless, without a shelter. But I have a house in a tree, too high for a normal person, but Mandy has nothing to lose. She always shares alcohol with me, because I'm not working at the moment.'

'Good news is that we can get some weed in Bearpitt after dark. And pills, and play chess with Noz.'

Two people on a walkway. Small path between rhythm and expression of melody. It's jazz plus eastern sound. High mountains test.

Wednesday.

BBC show of interpretations. Different scratch of code on the communication channel. Underground television, with a signal which is clear for a clear head. Squeeze brain with electric symulator beta soft.

To collect stuff from crash pad and remove it to the room without shooting anybody. I'm not sleeping because it's time for being unreal and on duty like a soldier. Watching around like a spy.

To hide from harassment of stereotypes and bad words, which sculpt reality without light inside.

'To light up a fire or create light is like, a basic human behaviour, innit?'

'Wicked man, oii!'

'Safe!'

'To serve and protect is a dog's task we hate the law it's killing our souls. To care for rules, social behaviour and isolation. Hundreds of voices are against it, to follow the leader, who see only to watch TV.'

'Tasty apple in the park, but it was poisoned with knowledge – so we have levelled up, building at higher level of spiritual experience.'

'I've lost my shoe…'

'I've lost my pill for dreams, just need to wait until breakdown.'

'Another panda was born in China – miracle of a dying species.'

Amelia Court for disabled person. Enlightened today and the last few months. I should go there and there, but I think I'm going nowhere. From there to that way. From here – there, like nowhere?

Anywhere. Anyway, it's not home yet. Home for the homeless – less & no home. Homeland. Land with home.

A landline with +48 to call somewhere.

'Leia, do you get it where I am?'

'Fuck off, especially you!'

'I can't get no satisfaction. I have no time for it. It's too late. I'm busy. I need a dictionary, it's all I need. So everybody fuck off, not just you…'

'You are in my head, but from the outside. I hear that you are calling me.'

'Not yet, you going to have a baby with the stranger, aren't you?'

'You fucking Polish twat!'

Leia's story is sad and her conversation with her ghost writer is done. We've met in a dancehall on an empty street during a fag break. Like a tea break - a break about five o'clock for a fag outside. Let's talk.

'What?'

'See you later Leia. Till Tuesday to play chess. See ya!'

'See ya. Bristol calling.'

'I always have calling from London, bye then.'

Next step was number four. It's a celebration. Your baby is my little student. Let's hold the kid till my birthday celebrations, I'll be a godmother. A daughter of a Polish Army colonel and a secret association and private society, working and shooting a guard / duty worker what ever you like.

If I'm alone, I feel Michael Jackson dancing in front of me, and other dead creatures. Like a zombie show – Pippshow Party 2013 with English subtitles.

Her sister on the block was Hidden Dragon/Mascotte Tiger. Volume, with electric drum'n'bass, Michael Jackson in a dance show with his reincarnated body, Bowie on saxophone and Mick Jagger.

I can't get no satisfaction in the air.

Next song is Don't Stop Me Now – with coke blown up from the kitchen table in a lovely sweep. I was thinking that I can't fall asleep, or I will be eaten by the death of Freddie Mercury, Madness, AIDS, the Club of 1986. A repeat from London and a Munich background with a short handled microphone, the African fight for Black rights, and the biggest gig in history. Never beaten – 1986.

'We'll play chess tomorrow Leia, bye.'

I've became an alien creation of a split personality, when my head broke in half and my brain shaved, in western film class B. But I've been reading western stories since I was a kid, watching the background on television or playing in the field with more than eighty per cent cowboys. I was a horse rider in a past life.

'Do you take your pills regularly Miss Steph?'

'Yes doc, regularly, but sometimes I forget a slice of bread. English bread of course, sir!'

'Indeed my young lady Fi. Your pattern of nature is ready too be taken on a frame.'

'Exactly dear prime minister, my painter is ready for your command, my lord.'

'Let's twist and shout! Battle for Britain! All invasions, Roman occupation and Viking blood in your veins, it made us conquerors. That's why the Scottish want to kill the English domination… My vision of a United Kingdom in the year 2013 is different. I have the power of creation. A power of coalition of allied nations to fight for the queen!'

'God Save The Queen! I wanna be ANARCHY!'

Sid Vicious was wicked! Too much heroin killed his body, but his music is still on the radio. Especially the Alien from Bristol Radio Station. Where the point of radar and the connection of a signal reader is situated on a Mont Blanc on top of the world.

'I said he's got really something.'

'I said I was right!'

'They say jump!'

'Jump they say! My friend, don't listen to them!'

At night, creatures are away, secured by robots and workers on night shift whose eyes have collapsed and are completely ruined like blankets on window.

Hidden eye contact has made a transmission to your brain and imagination.

To cover the wall with patterns and colour, an inspiration of a death experience or the LSD session in Switzerland last year.

Pure crystal of happiness and the allied forces of humans and gods and heroes with super creeps. An alien coalition of divorced strangers from strange dreams.

If they become unreal we will go to the hospital, like freaks on a leash.

I've been there once, I was fit to work an hour after they had locked my thoughts in a white pill and an injection to melt my psychosis in an observation room under CCTV on an uncomfy bed.

A girl who was tied to a bed and kept still and stable, was shouting with lust in her voice to fuck her harder.

She looked at me and I knew she would pick on me to be her slave.

It's shit man, but it's exciting if you have somebody around you. Ready to fuck you also, otherwise it's slavery. Bored and scared, to be eaten by Norman Bates' reincarnation or touched by the son of gods and a colour mix, changing from red through white to yellow and golden and light brown to the olive colour of outside. A side of a sculpture of a body.

His spirit has emanated as a happy rainbow with a bow and a gun.

Thursday.

Leia wants to have a conversation with dead painters and the famous reincarnations of Salvador Dali and Picasso and Basquiat. Even poppart is already to be seen in Bearpitt where it all began.

Warhol's poppart is now on television as a tea break. My reality become a truth, I'm not horrified that it's real and not only what I wanted in the past.

'It's like gods praying with a bottle of marihuana smoke.'

We are still fighting with the law to break the code to get upgraded to be superhuman – where is the glue of Universum? Where is the glue of sanity or the atomic structure of human's unique nature and a connection in society?

Later, about midnight, the creature appears in a garden. It was a thin hologram, cut and frozen like a photo of a ghost with dreadlocks, and chains on his neck. Black Ghost. African Ancestor.

I was a pirate then, all in all. I was a reincarnation of a shipowner trader trying to find a path on the ocean of Bristol.

I want to start a fight. With a dance section from 'Beat It', as a scratch, in this vision of our meeting. With beating drums in madman's hands. Like the magical moments of Great Aggression in Bearpitt last week, when I fell asleep, safe under the CCTV.

BOXCOIN. BEARpitt.

Drunken Irish Boy and Drunken Mandy, Chef Executive of Bearpitt. Private security and Occupy Bristol back in town. Please, we smoke one fag for five people here and listen to live music.

Set to play chess with some kind of Kasparov. He said I was cheating. Pfff!

'I have to drink coffee my dear.'

'It's cheap here.'

'Let's go to the house in the tree for a cuppa…'

'My home, they want to evict me. Ha! Ha!'

'This wine is strong and kicks my brain like a football shot. Mixed with coffee and skunk. They can't evict you. Now it's autumn, you need a tipi in Bearpitt. Home improvements and housing for a winter, Mandy.'

'Yeah, Occupy Bearpitt.'

We drink two wines with the boys on a site. I think I have psychosis, that this movie has become reality. It's a pub here, and free space for a night underground party. Is there Banksy somewhere? No, just Hunter S. Thompson with Johnny Depp's face. Completely pissed, Johnny becomes a Face from the Outside. Drunk Irish Boy, unemployed since he settled down in Britain, said to ask Hunter why he is here so long.

Kawasaki motor. Reading in Polish improves intelligence, upgrades existence level. But we Polish, we have to shut up and speak fluent English. So phase is made of a public bucket with a 41800 post code. So many thousand pounds I can make without tax. I will sell Kaiser balloons on a market, wearing clown's clothes.

Have to trip to Amsterdam for a cup. Nothing special. TV on screen this year, not very often, but realistic when I'm kicked in the eye with a must do action. Charger for a brain.

The brain is forced with pills and plant. Human brain upgraded to be supersonic, with the full vision of what is happening today. I've read it in a paper. Time travel to my past and suddenly I'm jumping to the future.

They want me to be slower, but I'm a superhero. This voice leads to domination and preparing for a death match.

We use secret code to hide our thoughts. We use the power of thoughts control – 'I've lost control.'

It's the voice of an old generation, playing new songs on a radio. It's the voice of aliens, hidden in superhuman bodies, sent by our ancestors, our KingDom roots.

Alien baby was already born from a woman's uterus, but died before Christ. This reincarnation is ready to reborn again. Slave is sold.

Free from stereotype vision on how to exist in a society of a town or a big city like London or New York or Warsaw. This trip is unfinished yet, but nowadays it's only poverty and sick pay, so I become a king off the throne.

I've lost my kingdom twice, but the land is still mine. I have a colony in my birthplace. I have a kingdom still. I have a sword in my pen. Pendrive. Find a future in magic cards, listen and connect with a goal during the VIP game. Not for losers, but we are a past generation. A few rebels and junkies with mental health problems, with a few anxiety symptoms and late schizophrenia. So take your meds, please.

Post from Royal Mail – it's been preselected by my friends' hands. My best friends.

Try to collect a thousand coins. In my bank account I can see nothing, but they don't believe me. Like it's a mouse trap and I am Hunter S. Thompson going for a fag. Bearpitt's got the face of Johnny Depp. I spend a lot of time staring into his aviators.

Underground rat race rest. Preparation to eat grass on the roundabout, in a mystery base. Hidden from eyes and CCTV. We can pretend we have this land forever. Squat an island. Conquer England without a fight. Dance section on Radio Bristol plays Daft Punk, it's traffic jam and interviews with reality. The night comes down. It's like *Zombie Horror Show*. I've become my thoughts, my creation, my past & my future.

Friday.

Payday, my account is empty. All I can do is to steal a picture, which I've found on a wall / screen. Freeze an impression, or feeling, to build a sculpture made of nothing but empty atoms. Post nuke war. Post nuke world. Fallout in my head, like a plant, it grows in space. I'm back in a game. Let's rock this house and city in my style. A ghost rider follows me I hardly recognise his steps. He lives in a closet, it's ready made and dead, but he wants something of mine.

We are the kings of Universe, we are king and queen. Are we heroes for one day only?

For next day, to survive in a wasteland. When my KingDom has collapsed, I've lost a throne and paradise and my wife in a castle. She is a widow. I'm here after a hundered divorces. Feel like a lonely dog from Tom Wolfe's subtitles novel. Long Short Story. Sometimes I feel lost. I don't know what time is, or a day, or a year.

It's payday, Friday 13th September 2013. Hope I didn't miss an appointment.

My present reincarnation of Salvador Dali wants me to paint his clocks and Human God Body.

I can create. I can see. I can watch through the wall. The Wall. On and on, again. Surrender the ego, pecunia non olet – money does not stink…

'Excuse me Sir/Madame have you got a fag or a spare pound? I'm collecting treasure to pay for my brain operation.'

'Sorry to hear that, but I've only got a card.'

'He's got a debt, my uncle. He will never rebuild the castle to make a wedding party. They think it's all joke, but a Polish joke. You'll never get it, there is too much history and too many dictionary meanings. It's boring for you my dear.'

The man is preparing my roll - up. I'm on my way to be happy for five minutes. Feeding my addiction, worst than a beggar.

We all have nice conversations, conversations to kill each other, without blood. Blood is too precious.

Suck a drop. It's free of hepatitis… - but I'm not sure, you never know. I'm already dead for two hundred years. My God made me to heal, but I'm more likely to destroy. I have my owners deep in my mind. To turn on an engine I need fuel. Need to stop all addictions, quit with toxins and quit with life I think.

I'm a fucking train in slow motion. Frozen in a nightmare. Filled with the shadows of my past lives. I've lost my KingDom. I am enlightened with thoughts. I am just another brick in the wall. Fuck/Kurwa.

Early in the morning there was a bomb alarm in the city. Planes stopped, train tracks were destroyed. We had to escape, but had no idea where to go.

We run off to an Island, where it is safe. Cracked head, to take some heroin, in a better place.

High level of excitement and anxiety. Fire on Babylon!

My brain reached the goal to stay uncounscious when it's dark. It's the most dangerous moment, it's a state of war!!!

Radio still plays sexy songs about love, but we all know it's bull shit, or fake film to cover a scam. To provide so called accomodation for thoughts. When I'm unable to move, to dance, under attack with bombs made of gas. Gas from Russia. From Afghanistan or Polish Mountains. Secretly taken from Moon, to kill freedom.

I left my KingDom, because of my father, he is on a trip, he forgot the language and he lost his keys to the castle. An empty village grows around an empty defence construction. It's built with super resistant blocks of a cosmic substance and covered with pulses of energy concentrated in the middle. A scratched hologram of a white witch is the only one left on duty, but we were allied with our closest neighbours, so we are protected as kings of this land.

Another hour without my kingdom. I left the house last spring and I hadn't much time to find the grave of the baby alien. We met last year, he was already born, but now it's time to meet his mother.

I'm trying to make eye contact with her, but she is in a cave, like Plato. Sees only shadows of her past lives, when she was a mother. Now she is only a shadow painted on a wall, with blind eyes covered by the dust of medication. The levels of medication heal the hole of her suffering and keep her anxiety deep in a cave with male and female faces multiplied, like the eyes of fly. She is surrounded by the cloned faces of males who tell her what to do each day, but she is tired. We drink tea and have a conversation, about death experience and poverty, about lack of happiness.

'I think, I'm going to my cave to keep an eye on my baby.'

'Can you connect with the cave easily?'

'I'm in a cave already.'

'I was a radio station and TV listener before. Now, I have power to control the signal, to not come directly to my mind. I can see things which normal people can't see. Electric ships under fire, the fight of foreigners and wars.'

'I'm gonna die soon.'

'You won't die tomorrow, not yet. See this line on your hand? It means you have another trip on the way.'

She swallows pills and her kingdom comes again.

Conception of Alien Baby, born in a cave a long, long time ago.

We are in the same age in real bodies, but our mind powers contain past creations. I can see that Plato cave where Leia lives and I will scratch the walls like an artist to cover them with my vision.

We smoke holy plant to enter into the cave. We share the smoke with others around, shadows and guests, ghosts riders. The cave is filled with a crowd of male ghosts. We sit completely stoned. The cave is made of gold and I started a fire. A ghost rider covers my spirit, I'm not afraid. It's the shadow of my spirit power, my ancestor and my angel. He protects my soul against bad luck, or bad haze, which comes from the sacred scratch of the underground. The toxic gas of the devil's grave.

Devil is sleeping in a pill, Zopiclone, The Great Doc keeps an eye on this naughty boy who tries to start psychotherapy. God has won this neverending fight with good and bad. Conception of mind upgrade, to be in a safe pleasures garden, brings us to the point of eating an apple.

Few secret gardens contain fresh fruits which lead us to temptation, to feed our veins with the forbidden juice of knowledge and freedom.

Not yet. Not now, but I've already realised that this history never ends.

It's a fucking circle, it's a suffering for my lively soul. The cave is full of music,

filled with drums and bass rythm, filled with holy smoke. I'm deep in a haze, watching shadows on the wall. It's only an illusion. I can control my vision, but Leia is happy.

Everybody realises the second step, the next chapter, the next myth and the next psychosis consequences.

My mind is connected with the cave in the Mystic Garden of Madhouse on our street.

Last apple on the tree, who will eat it?

Better, I'll set up a playlist for Radio Alien.

Old tunes which dominate the air are forever to remind of the past. We live in a circle.

This year we will conquer England. To be kings of the Universe, to live in a better place.

'Did you pay tax before you died?'

'Not yet, my lord. I've lost my treasure. I was beaten, when I was hopeless and alone. My companions drank the juice of profit. I've lost my kingdom. I have to break the spell.'

Chapter Two.

NN cementary. Cherie's tent is watched by a German shepherd. Living with the dead. Watching her sleeping on a methadon programme. Her ghost rider reads her books, wears her clothes, but she is asleep. Away from home. Scary for living creatures, never to appear after dark, even with dogs.

No Jesus here, just old oaks and the windy whisper of my mother's grave. Living with ghosts, and animals, and ghost riders and hidden thoughts.

Her boyfriend meets me sometimes, somewhere around the backyard. On a big scale it's quite a big garden hidden in the town centre, it's the middle of the Midlands. It's a point.

'Of course, a point of view. I'm on a methadone programme.'

'I can see.'

'I've been in Barrywood Asylum.'

'Me too, you want a fag?'

We lie in a house under a tree, hidden, like in a state of war in 1980, when I was born in Poland, not yet free. But still.

Millions of eyes control the city, police CCTV is elsewhere, but not here. Safe, without GPS and the control of microphones, we could talk as normal.

On a graveyard, between the sleeping dead of reunited mothers and daughters, First World War soldiers, who died for NN.

Lost Kingdom. Destroyed city and all is in a museum. Shoes and brewing, home of industry. used to be an awesome working class hero a high level of awesome. Level up. Upgrade in NN Museum of Shoes, where I've been locked up at night, after tea time. Too much weed.

I felt trapped at night in the museum with shoes made by this town of sleepers and coco nuts. Middle main city - the London part in the next two hundred years, tube for three pounds. If not, should be.

Maybe Virgin Trains already made it, but it's too posh for us.

'I'm not so desperate. Last time I was travelling to Hounslow it was sixteen hours through Oxford! And I met Scrappy from London. I paid for a ticket, only three pounds, but I spent for illegal drugs plenty.'

'Is he here next Wednesday, on a market?'

'Yes, we are supposed to meet there next Wednesday, but I was at a party in Hounslow. I think I was in Surrey too.'

'For a cup of tea with whom?'

'With boredom. The flat was worth over million pounds. Covered with moondust. I was told by the Polish guard that he keeps an eye on everything like CCTV and I believe him. Polish guards are more active at night. Like eagles. A white one from Polish lands, but luckily on foreign sand, we just check how it is outside and we miss a lot more, like the romantic poets of the Second Great Escape two hundred years ago. We fly away to make extra checks. Like idiots without any goal. Just miss, and watch for shit money...'

'You are right, we are twats. That's why we are abroad. We are last in the class, but we are fast abroad ahead off other twats! Ha ha!'

'Yes, and we know the history and we are television watchers from the eighties haha. I'm well prepared to be an English twat. We are stars in a dope show! The words become reality. I think my Great Escape has been made. I'm a time traveller. Gypsie and Jude on a great walk of survivors.'

Yes, it's already made. My own words for everything that was done. I think that play is written.

I wish to write more about girls who live around me. And some boys from the past, but I think this should be the next chapter. Now I'm on a beer with Cherie and her boyfriend, in a tent in a graveyard. On the other side of the road is St. Andrews Asylum for nuts. This town offers full service for everybody, except for a tube. A small town in the middle of nowhere. Everybody on pills, sleeping, like in a nightmare. The worst is night shift, when creatures come out alive. My doc says I have to sleep more, but how am I meant to sleep when the worst comes at night?

Everybody crisps. I woud like to make a crazy party for my old friends, but just realised - that I'm alone for a very long time. Love is gone, left me without any reason. My kingdom is gone.

I feel like I am in a film. I feel I'm in a game, I have lost my army, a whole division of my friends. They are somewhere. My army has expired. Out of date. War is over.

My plastic card has got no gold to pay for soldiers and expenses. I wish I could meet the ghosts of rebels to make them help me. I think I have some hidden treasure in Engand, but the Scot betrayed me. He ran away with my gold. My silver heart is gone. I have no heart. I have nothing except the power of my creation. Wish I had my ring to recall my ancestors, to find a path on a sea full of sharks.

Help me Hanuman, help me Krishna, help me to get back my kingdom.

Pray. The only thing that's left. Pray.

I'm alone in a sweet garden to watch sun-beams eating nature. Somewhat rainy, and a little rainbow runs through my eyes, makes a connection with God's mind.

I'm not in a garden anymore. This sweet illusion of happiness is real - I'm filled with sun, eating golden flakes for early breakfast, and drinking mystery herb juice to reveal holograms.

My fantastic body has fallen asleep in a garden in the rain, but my mind is in a Great Hall with a purple haze.

The dead are watching me without being scary. I am not scared anymore. I'm too proud to be scared. Besides, human fears are left in the mystery garden with living people.

My king sits in front of me in the company of men and women. Each one has got a shiny sword and a cup of red wine produced in France for god's only. It's a posh drink only for superheroes and them.

I have an opportunity to drink with them, I'm blue. I'm their son and their daughter. I'm their King on Earth with a mission to rebuild the Great Kingdom. We share wine and the plant pipe to grow. We all grow.

Gods and my ancestors meet me, surround me and a thousand years pass like an hour. We talk about life, we talk about what is my target? It's a secret, to find the Holy Grail. To find a magic spell and my lost heart, which turned into a silver stone.

My human body coexists with spirits and plants from the secret garden. I am still alive. Another life has been saved.

In Polish mental hospitals money goes on sugar, coffee and fags. Emergency tobacco. I got the munchies. My stomach is like elephant, eats a mouse and nothing. Blocks, pictograms of music, falling Lego blocks. A castle with waterfalls builds itself with towers. Soldiers, knights, magician and Chef, right from hospital. A printed face in a hologram of a water bottle. This was my oasis on the bottom of the sea. Indeed.

No men allowed on that side, please!

Fuck off!

Look out, not that side, haha!

We drink coffee and smoke fags like a female gang, with a Michael Jackson soundtrack in the background. Live:

Beat it! Beat it! Bearpitt!

Brain operation.

Someone called the police to keep us in a closet. We tried to run, but we hide in the nearest closet in my room. Sun-beams dance on the floor. Rainbow. Nothing on TV, only running ants. ANTS after coffee. Four shots of espresso like I used to. To kill the liver. And charge blood in my veins.

'Smokin fags?'

'Would you go to the garage?'

'She wasn't allowed to buy fags. She looks minor.'

I look like a rockstar in my head. It's ridiculous I know. On a radio, The Beatles.

Polish police. Poles abroad. Soldiers and policemen.

'Tomorrow I will have six hundred pounds, but tomorrow...'

'I've got only two pounds, so let's rock this town with a bottle of cider!'

We were mad, we were pissed, we had a total eclipse!

With lines of cocaine and crack hits in the living room. Than we found good and bad books. Forbidden even nowadays. To show the truth.

'Doc will send me to a mental hospital to take a rest. I am so pissed off...'

'Yeah!'

'I miss peace, and social care with free fags. They told me to not use Facebook, to not inform anybody that I am in the happy house. I sent information straight away saying where I was when I entered to FB. I was waiting for phone calls or strange visitors but no-one has come. Only a crazy party in a dance hall where there is psychosis.'

I thought it was a game, but it was real, that crap again. I was thinking that I'm locked up in the prison of my head. Forever, if I won't recall my memory.

I was taken to the escalation room when I was playing drums on the door like a rasta. The security and black nurse took me to the room, I already had lost the power to hide my thoughts about my dead mother. I hit first time. Nothing.

Divorce was done. After all. I feel free.

Microphones and CCTV have been switched - off for a tea, or coffee, if you like. This movie is still on and on in my life. Now it's real. Life is real.

Later, when it gets dark, the lights on the streets are making noises with bulbs made of glass. Not soda bulbs, electric button ON/OFF, on a link with sound.

'Corridor is cut with automatic doors. The doors.'

"I'm passing through glass. Hop Hop!'

Meeting with Holly, the Wednesday afternoon before Friday.

I went to the Wild Goose to eat a proper meal and was served chicken drumsticks and mashed potatoes with sauce and some salad, and a pie, and juice as well. I sat down not far from the sharp bisexual woman with a hat on.

Then Holly Grrrl enters the restaurant with a backpack. I have finished reading advertisements for jobseekers, rolled a roll - up on a sofa.

I was thinking about coffee while rolling my roll - up, but the girl disappeared somewhere, after she ate her pie. Sexy and nice I wonder how she is smoking fags.

She comes back at one stage ready to go to the front of the building. I'm picking up my ass, lifting whole body to the door, to go outside. We are smokin' fags and we talk I smile at her, she is in a company of guys from Bearpitt.

'How you doin'? Nice haircut. Nice colours. What's your name?'

'Holly, and yours?'

'Fighter of the tribe, is German root of my name, coupled with Hungarian queen of salt miners, originally from Poland.'

'I am also German. Half- German by my father, half - Uruguay by my mother. I was born in Uruguay a long time ago.'

We travel from the town to the city. Town centre, from Easton through Old Market – queer city with it's rainbow united bars where I have to come back later. We struggle to find a place to stay for a spliff. Near boats. Before she reaches the railway station, so we haven't got much time.

Most of the boys disappeared into shadows of the past.

We keep our feet in the water, so I saw her socks. One with stripes and red hearts, and one black with colour spots. Nice composition, the most marvellous being a big hole in the heel. So cute. Size six or seven, she doesn't know. Relaxing over the water, quite dirty, but the only river here.

If you can't beat them – join them!

'Wicked, year 2013. No-one had any authority. This is the answer to all questions.'

'You've got plenty of questions?'

'Yes, all subcultures are coming up. Underground appears.'

We have many authority answers. We are fuckin lucky. We are the history. We are making the future. Not just floating by, passing. But it is a form of collective counsciouseness, to do collective things or have collective ideas.

'We purely care for having an experience. Slow down, to catch up with a sense, a feeling.'

'This can be exciting.'

We smoked a spliff already mixed with hash and weed, so the conversation becomes more mystic. 'Everytime we smoke together, it's like God blesses us around our heads. I believe in this sort of god's creation of a visioner's voice. Like an upgrade of the mind. Only the god can smoke all the time, but it's risky. In Nepal, where I will be next year in the summer, you can buy weed for two pounds and it will last for a whole month. I will pay twice for visas to travel longer, maybe half a year. What you think?'

'Good point. Make a party on Mount Everest.'

'No, I will only travel there to spend all night and all day on top of the world, ma.'

'I know who it is. It's magic. I can see her face. It's an alien woman with super powers. You are a special agent with cameras in your eyes. You're a policewoman. Catwoman and Batman's daughter in one. And your clothes are special. You're from Gotham City, in London?'

My magic coat left in NN. My Batman's cover plate, and camera in London. I have some payments next week so I can buy a ticket to London to meet Batman. My father in law.

'Doing is nothing else.'

A boat is approaching like a ship, but it's a ferry. Few people left the ferry, but I was focused on my spliff, to smoke it with a passion and hold the smoke so long in my lungs, and not to lose it. To keep my psychosis ON.

My psychosis is art. It's a war in my head. Like I was in prison, to see inside. Fight from the inside, fight it for real. So real. Socreality. Socialism reigned in Britain. Free weed for the masses.

We can mix original music of the eighties and 2013 and make a new sound of Bristol. This will be a big hit in England or even the rest of the world. To wake up the dead. Think of it. To create a Book of Dead. To meet their reincarnation. Shapes and new masks. They can do something other than rest in peace.

'In your music – you can be free. If you are happy you can make your own music, if you're not happy there is no point.'

'I've got a long way to go.'

'You can't be fuckin' leader/dealer if you are not happy enough…'

'Not to be active – it's like a near death experience. It's a death.'

'Should we go somewhere?'

'Where?'

'I don't know…'

She wears a bright pink scarf and a brown sweater with sky-blue stripes. Carrots in a foil bag fresh and tasty, crunchy. The sweater's stripe was making an impression of concentric spirals on her tits. It looks like a snake, or a line to heaven.

'I'm thinking how to organise my own music and a big festival. I know some places to do it. I know some people who know some people, blah blah.'

'I know some also. I have my own vision. Mixer Eighties and 2013 and futurist sci-fi in music, live on black records. Mixer?'

The Special K cider is almost empty. I took one sip and that's it. The rest disappeared while Holly went for a pee, faster than a man. I have her phone number so I'm secure. She said she will be here in two weeks time. She works for festivals sometimes, so I asked her to be my manager. I will show her my music. We had a spliff in cinema projection darkness.

Holly vs Uruguay boy with German blood.

'Try experience. I don't, I live through my consciousness.'

'Everybody has got different goals in life.'

She stopped to play guitar. A couple of royal swans swam to meet us with angry, hungry eyes. Holly feeds them with the carrots and they float away, the carrots swim in the dirty water as orange points, shining through green water. The swans are angry and nasty, they want to get some food. We sing protest songs with Bob Marley in the air. Radio Freedom plays Buffalo Soldier.

Adidas Generation.

All in blue and red and pink. Factory of trainers. My uncle's got a shoe factory in Switzerland. I've got QC experience. He can give me a job. This is my poem – my CV. My blood and sweat. My experience at work.

I am planning my next trip – outside. To jump from the Suspension Bridge. To the cold water, with Jim Morrison and his Hotel California, from a sunrise in a dessert. Like Indiana Jones with superpowers. I am watching the alien's invasion.

I am sorry for any inconvenience. I am sorry. Like an original Polish person. We complain all the time, about weather, sickness, bad luck.

'Hi, how are you?'

'Oh, man. My life is so shit! I can't stand it anymore. I am leaving NN. Got to catch the wind in my hair. Some fresh air. Some fresh points of view. New categories. Hopefully it won't be a dinner with dead God. Oh, my firend. It's socrealism, money for nothing and chicks for free. I've got a contract with a big company in town. I have nothing to lose. Have to earn some money. I need a million in my account. I will be rich. I can start to break the law more securely. As a politician or an artist. I can break rules. As a hero of the working class. People from the factory chose me for a mission up there.'

After all, my brain was washed and shaved off fat. In brain powder there are active atom structures which activate or deactivate some parts of the human brain. It depends which powder is used to wash memory, and if it's for long or short term. I feel like a child in Hazelwood Road, no language, no history, no memories. I am zero. I am nobody. I speak with no original tongue. I talk without my own cultural context. I converse without literate patterns. Like a poor, made in China, only to work like a meat.

Blood from the heart.

And all fluids to keep the organism alive and active.

My empty brain has been resuscitated.

I was completely Deleted and now I am ready and have spare space for new data. Installation in progress. Please take a seat to complete the task before midnight.

We can ask if we are more happy without our thoughts involved in the revolution. Mental revolution. This new society. A new background is ready to be active, for a long time. We are the nations united, we are the tribes in basics. Like medieval ancestors, like survivors after the Great Battle. This war is over. One coffee please, to charge me up again.

Printed in Great Britain
by Amazon